VICIO

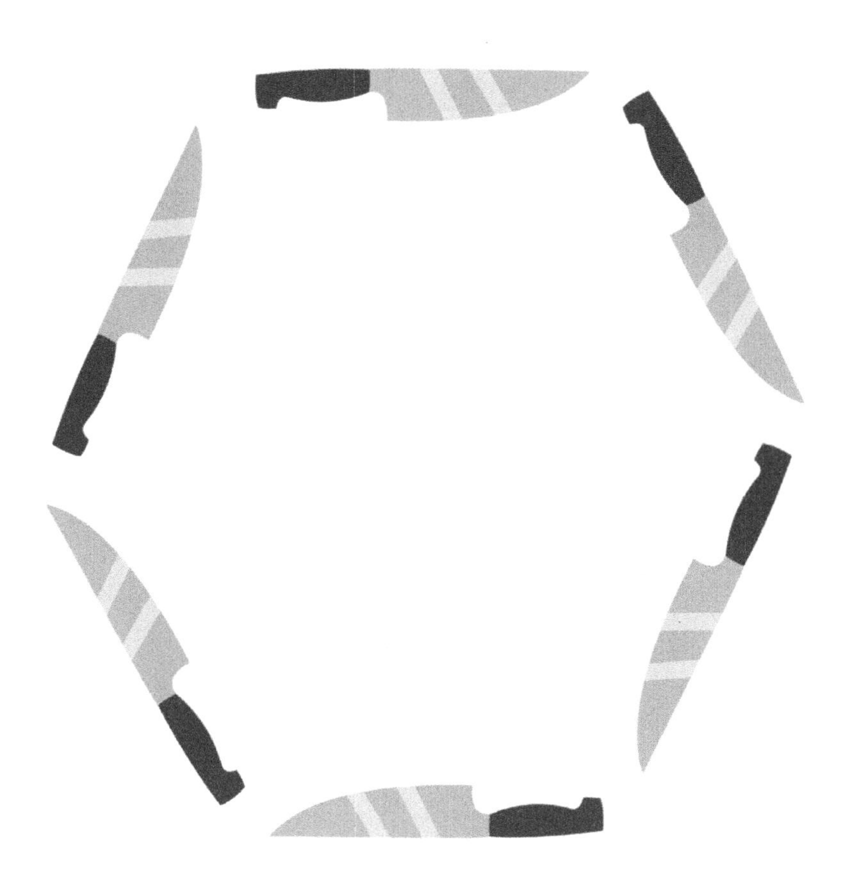

South VC

Thank you to

A whole bunch of wacky teens who are addicted to 7-11,

The loving person who gave birth to me,

Distant family close to my heart,

The most amazing humans I have ever met,

And coffee.

TABLE OF CONTENTS

Chapter 1

When I was eight, I began riding the bus on my own. I almost never used it to genuinely go anywhere, only using it as an alternative to being at home. I would rather do my homework on a bumpy bus than be interrupted by beer cans being thrown at my head or being yelled at to do whatever chore my stepmother thought was fit to keep me out of the way.

I made somewhat-friends on my bus adventures, whether it was with the bus drivers, or the riders I saw almost every day. Either way, I knew I was safe since the drivers always made sure I got home before it was too dark. They went out of their way to get me home, which I appreciated, but I did feel bad about it.

After I graduated from high school at ten, I worked hard to get my Private Investigator's license. When I began getting cases, I would bring my laptop on the bus and use a hotspot on my phone so I could work on them.

I often brought my laptop and would work on cases while on the bus. After I graduated from high school at the age of ten, I went on to take

some college courses so I could get my Private Investigator license. If the bus was empty, sometimes I would ask the driver what they would think of the case

I was working on at the time, and we would go back and forth on theories.

As soon as I was eligible to enter a course for my learner's permit, I signed up without a second thought. My family barely saw me after I bought my first car. Being on the road, or even just in my vehicle, gave me this sense of peace. It calmed my nerves, and strangely inspired me to work harder and more efficiently. At times, I would even park in a random lot and work there. I felt much better being alone, and I hardly ever felt lonely.

But loneliness is more of a concept, I find. Many people find comfort in being on their own, perfectly content with the quiet of their mind. Others need people and conversation to drown out the screaming in their head. However, both types of people would feel alone in a room full of people. That I knew for certain.

That's another reason why I loved driving. On the road, you could be in your own space, still surrounded by hundreds of other people, and yet you'd still be alone. I had found comfort in

the rumbles and shakes of the engines, and I didn't plan on letting go of it just yet.

But that day I wasn't driving for fun. That day was a whole two weeks after my eighteenth birthday, so I finally moved out and into a new city. I had been planning on it for the last 3 years because it was *that* important. It was the final goodbye to my rotten parents. I was at last on my own after 18, long years. The best part was that my family couldn't get pissed and say I was moving because I hate them. I had the luck of saying the new city had "better job opportunities."

I had every aspect all set, knowing exactly what would come next, and I wasn't going to let anything mess it up. Everything was organized and neat. Just as everything should be.

I arrived in the new city at exactly 6:34 pm. I drove to my new apartment and parked around the area.

The cold nipped at my nose as soon as I opened my door. The snow crunched beneath my boots as I stepped out, and I tried to hurry with gathering the rest of my things quickly to

avoid frostbite. I locked my car and headed for the front door.

Once inside my apartment, I took my time to unpack and fashion everything to my standards; Reorganizing all the placeholder furniture that came with the pad, placing my abstract paintings in order of abstractness, and hanging my certificates of accomplishment according to date.

The last thing to unpack was my laptop. I pulled it out of my bag and set it up on my new desk, then took a seat. I carefully opened my laptop and waited for it to start up, closing most of the tabs I had open as soon as it did. After relaxing, working on my blog, and reading some articles about whatever piqued my interest, a ping sounded from my PC. An Email.

I opened my email and click on the newest one, not recognizing the sender.

Harriet Hanks <hahaimfunny@email.com>

Subject: Please Help

My name is Harriet Hanks, and recently my brother has gone missing. His name is Abe, he's 18, and he was last seen on the 4th. I just need your help. Please, please help me. And I know you just moved into my city because of your blog, so don't try and act like you can't work this case. Please.

I thought critically. The job interested me, I could not deny that. A missing person always was interesting, even if it sometimes ended darkly. But it was a job more suited for police detectives, not a private detective such as me. The temptation was hard to resist, but I replied.

K McIntyre <detectivekmcintyre@email.com>

Re: Please Help

I would suggest going to the police for such a matter, not a private detective.

Harriet Hanks <hahaimfunny@email.com>

Re: Please Help

I don't trust the police. Please. I'm begging you. I have the money to pay you, I just want my brother back.

I sighed and argued back and forth with myself, weighing the options. I could meet with this person and evaluate if it was worth my time, and if not, I would convince her to go to the police.

K McIntyre <detectivekmcintyre@email.com>

Re: Please Help

Fine. We may meet up to further discuss this, but I really believe that this would be best handled by the proper police.

Harriet Hanks <hahaimfunny@email.com>

Re: Please Help

YES!! Thank you! Thank you thank you thank you thank you thank you! We can meet at my house tomorrow.

I reluctantly agreed to this proposition and she gave me her address. We quickly exchanged phone numbers, and I spent the rest of my night researching Abe and Harriet Hanks. I didn't find much, just articles on their school's sports teams.

To be perfectly honest, I was more interested in the idea of the case than I was in solving it.

Missing people always intrigued me, even more than murder, because sometimes the person is never found. With murder, you know how it ends. You just have to recount everything that happened. With a missing person, there was no way to tell. You had to figure out the story by yourself.

However, I may have a slight bias towards missing person cases because of what Roman once said to me.

"Missing people are like stories that sometimes never finish. We don't even know if they ever end. They could

be like a poem, never truly complete; They just stop moving."

Chapter 2

I opened the gate in front of the three-story, modern home before me. Walking the short distance to the front door, I noticed the myriad of Christmas decorations still left up in the yard, even after the holiday had passed. I stepped up to the front door and onto the welcome mat, which read "HANKS" in big, bold, cursive letters. The doorbell made a buzzing sound as I pressed down on it.

Not a moment later, I heard faint footsteps run to the door and swing it open. In the doorway stood an average sized teenage girl with pastel pink hair. Her green eyes widened upon seeing me. "Oh! You're here early!"

I looked down at my watch. "I'm exactly on time."

"Yeah, early. Anyway, I'm Harriet." She stuck her hand out to greet me. I gave it a slight shake.

"I'm K, but you obviously already knew that," I said as I stepped inside, closing the door behind me.

As I took my boots off, from a distance, I heard an older woman call out, "Harriet, who's at the door?"

"Just a friend from school, Mom!" The pink haired girl replied.

"Excuse me?" I gave her a confused look.

An older gentleman rounded the corner and looked at both of us. "Would your friend like some cookies? What's her favorite kind?" He asked kindly.

Harriet rolled her eyes. "She doesn't want cookies, Dad."

I was about to say something, but she grabbed my hand and dragged me upstairs to her room before I could even get a word in.

Once there, she let go of my hand and turned to face me. "Listen, this will sound weird but—"

"Your parents don't know that your brother is missing, do they?"

"What? How did you know? We didn't talk about that over e-mail."

"The way your parents questioned who was at the door lead me to believe that they

weren't aware someone was coming over today, nevertheless someone coming to investigate their missing son. Then you told your mother I was a friend from school, which is suspicious like you didn't want her to know who I was. Finally, yesterday, over e-mail, you mentioned not trusting the police, which I earlier suspected to be some kind of lie, and I was correct. It's not that you don't trust them, you just don't want them involved, because you don't want your parents figuring out your brother is missing."

Her eyes widened. "Whoa. You are good."

I shrugged. "Now the only question is, why are you keeping it a secret?"

She sighed, and her voice became measurably quieter, "Abe told my parents that he was going on a school trip, and he even got them to sign these forms, but it was all fake. He wasn't on a school trip, he went on a mini-vacation with his boyfriend."

"Ah," I nod, "and he hasn't come out to your parents yet."

She looked down and nodded, some hair previously tucked behind her ear fell in front of one eye. "Neither of us have. But his boyfriend called two days ago and asked if Abe came back home. I told him, no, and he said that he and Abe got into a fight and he stormed out or something. No one has seen Abe since, but my parents still think he's on a school trip."

She looked up at me, her expression only reading desperation. "I am literally begging you, please help me find him, but don't tell my parents. They can't know about any of this."

I stood for a moment, hand on my chin. "I'm processing it. I'm thinking. Weighing consequences. I'm intrigued," I nodded and stuck my hand out. "I accept."

Her eyes widened, her shoulders visibly relaxing. "Oh, thank god," she shook my hand excitedly.

I sat down on her bed and pulled out a notepad and pen, quickly writing down all the details she previously mentioned.

"Is there any family or friends you think Abe could have run off to?"

"No, Abe doesn't like most of the people in our school, and we don't have any aunts or uncles."

"Grandparents?"

"One set passed away two years ago, and the other lives in Hawaii."

"What's his boyfriend's name?"

"Nico. Nico Ruiz."

"Good. Our next step is to speak to him. Where would he be at this time of day?"

"Probably still at school. He has volleyball practice by now."

"Then that's where we head."

"What? No more questions?"

"Not for you, no. Let's go."

I stood up and started striding for the door, Harriet following close behind. We left the house, and as we were leaving, I noticed the Christmas decorations once again.

"Your family really should take those decorations down," I commented.

"Those are up year-round." She replied, swinging her arms at her side.

"… You're kidding."

"Nope. My family owns a skating rink franchise -- You've probably seen the billboards? Hanks Skates, where it's always Christmas!" She did a mock-preppy voice, then rolled her eyes.

I raised my eyebrows. "Yikes."

We hopped in my car and she directed me to her school, where, upon arrival, we headed straight for the gymnasium.

Sneaker squeaks and the slapping sounds of volleyballs hitting the floors echoed through the small gym. Boys hit balls back and forth over the net, only a select few noticing us enter. A tall man with a whistle dangling around his neck approached us.

"Harriet," he nodded to her, and she shyly waved back. "How can I help you two?" He inquired, scratching his handlebar mustache.

"My name is K McIntyre, I'm a private detective," I pulled out my P.I license and a business card, handing to them to him. "I just need to ask Nico Ruiz some questions for a case."

He quickly examined my credentials and turned to one end of the gym. "Nico!"

A boy with black hair and tan skin turned his head to look at us, almost getting hit with a ball in the process. He ducked to avoid it and ran speedily over to us.

"Yeah?"

"This is Detective McIntyre, she'd like to ask you some questions..." He gestured to me, but his voice dripped with skepticism.

We made eye contact, and he didn't seem confused in the slightest. He also seemed to know who I was, as he trusted me immediately when I asked him to follow me. We walked out of the gymnasium and into the hallway where Harriet lead us to an empty classroom. I took a seat and pulled out my notepad and pen, readying a new page.

He slid into a chair in front of me. "So… Harriet really did contact you."

I glanced at him, then at Harriet, who stood by sheepishly.

"She did. For the record, I recommended that you go to the police, but I can't force you to do anything."

He nodded and leaned back in the chair.

"So, Nico, as I understand, you are Abe Hanks' boyfriend?"

"Yeah, I am." He twiddled with his fingers and picked at the black nail polish on his nails.

"And you were also the last person to see him?"

"Well, the staff from the motel we were staying at might have seen him leave."

I wrote that down.

"Walk me through the last time you saw him."

"Okay… Um, well, it was around three or four in the afternoon. We were just sitting around, talking, and we started to get into an argument."

"What was the argument about?"

He looked away, seemingly embarrassed.

"I was mad because he still hadn't come out to his parents, which I know is super selfish, but it's been bothering me."

"What happened after that?"

"Well, I packed up my stuff, and I left Abe some money so he could get home. Then I called a cab and went back to my house. He yelled at me as I left the room and tried to get me to stay, but I haven't seen him since."

"So, you left him there?" I raised an eyebrow.

His cheeks reddened. "Yeah… It was a super shitty thing to do to, I know, and I feel really bad about it, especially now, but the fight got, like, super personal. It was awful. I just had to leave."

I simply nodded my head as I wrote, rarely looking up.

"What was the name of the motel?"

"Um, Marie Enn Motel. It's not far outside the city, we just wanted somewhere farther away than a fortuitous hotel near our homes."

My pen scratched the paper as I wrote that down and circled it thrice. "Now, that was far over 24 hours ago, why didn't you file a missing person report?"

"I was going to after I contacted Harriet to ask her if he got home safe, and she said she hadn't seen him since he first left. But she told me not to because she didn't want to get the police involved. If we did, then she'd have to explain the whole thing to her parents and they'd find out that Abe had a boyfriend, therefore outing him. And because Harriet has a need for the spotlight," he looked back at Harriet and glared a little. "she'd out herself as well."

My eyes glanced over to her as well and saw her wounded expression.

"That's not even…" She halted her sentence and looked away, clearly trying

to stop any kind of tears from coming up.

I turned back to Nico and continued interrogating him.

"Did anyone else know about the trip?"

"No one. I only told Harriet Bout it after Abe went missing."

"Did anyone have some sort of vendetta against Abe at any point? Anyone at all?"

He shakes his head. "No. No one I can think of."

"Was he acting strangely before your trip? Did he feel like something was off?"

"He seemed perfectly fine. To me, anyway. And he tells me about everything."

Harriet scoffed like some kind of heckler. I sighed and looked at her.

"Would you care to leave? You're being *quite* distracting."

She furrowed her brows and stormed out. "Whatever."

I turned back to Nico, whose expression turned a tad smug. I figured he and Harriet must have had some type of rivalry for Abe's attention and ignored it.

"Let's continue."

I spent a good five minutes picking Nico's brain about him, his relationship with Abe, his relationship with Harriet, and more. Weirdly, the more I knew about him, the less I trusted. I would say I didn't know why, but I did. I had an idea why. An impossible, unrealistic, stupid idea that wouldn't have gotten the investigation anywhere if let myself believe it. So, I didn't.

I let Nico go back to his volleyball practice and Harriet and I left.

She clicked her seatbelt together, then turned to me. "Where to next?"

"Well, I want to check Abe and Nico's alibis at the motel."

"Cool, so we'll head up there and then—"

"You're not coming." I interrupted.

"What?" She pouted. "What the hell? Why not?"

"To be frank, I'm a professional. I don't have a use for someone who isn't."

"I can be professional!"

"Really. I'd love to see that." I rolled my eyes, but she continued to plead.

"I know more about both of them than you do! I'll be able to tell you immediately if something is off."

"I'm not saying that isn't true… but…"

"But what? I can be helpful! Besides, it'll be nice to have some company, won't it?"

"I prefer being alone."

"That's just what lonely people say to make themselves feel better."

"I disagree."

"Okay, but you still gotta take me with you! Please? Please?"

"You're acting much too excited about this. You don't even seem concerned about your brother," I narrowed my eyes, "which is rather suspicious."

"I just want to help solve a mystery for once... And not get treated like a little kid..."

It's almost embarrassing to admit that that is what persuaded me to let her join the hunt. I empathized a little too much with her resent for being treated like a child. I couldn't count the number of times someone had underestimate me because of my age. I bit my lip gently, then rolled my eyes.

"Fine."

She gasped happily. "Really?! Yes! Thank youuuu!!" She probably would have reached over to hug me if I hadn't started the car and began driving already. "But can we stop by my house anyway? I've been to that motel, it's kind of a long drive. We should grab snacks and stuff."

I sighed and gave in, heading to her house. Harriet wasn't often right, but in this case, she was right about one thing; It would be a long drive.

Chapter 3

Harriet hummed along to some pop song on the radio as she perused a magazine she brought along. I really didn't see the point of those silly magazines, but I wouldn't dare say anything about it. Eventually, she sat back and sighed loudly.

"I'm bored," she said, despite having clearly expressed that already.

"You were the one who wanted to come along."

"I know, but I didn't think being a detective would be this boring." She complained sophomorically.

My eyes would have rolled to the back of my head if I didn't have enough self-control to keep them still. It was one, tiny, two-hour drive and she whined like some small, hapless infant.

She huffed and looked out her window, leaning away from me like an angry girlfriend. "It would be a lot less boring if you would actually talk to me."

"Well, you didn't engage in conversation either!" I defended.

"Yes, I did! I asked what your favorite type of chips are!"

"And I very clearly stated that I don't partake in the consumption of potato chips because of their high sodium content."

She groaned and rolled her eyes so fiercely that I thought they were going to pop out of her skull. "Wouldn't kill you to have some fun."

"We have completely different descriptions of fun."

"Oh, yeah?" If her voice was any more condescending, she would have choked. "What do you like to do for fun?"

"I read mystery novels."

"What about unsolved mysteries?" She pulls a large but thin, black book out of her bag. The title was in bold, red letters, but I didn't have time to read it all, as I had to focus on not crashing my car into a ditch. "This is my favorite book of all time." She explained, the smile on her face almost incomparable. "I read it at least once a week."

I wanted to complain so badly. I wanted to tell her that I don't like personal conversations

and that she should stay completely professional with me. There wasn't anything stopping me. I didn't care if someone thought I was rude. But just the thought of saying that to her felt like stealing candy from a child old enough to eat candy. So, I sucked it up and responded.

"Why?" I asked with an accidentally snide tone.

That's why I never socialized.

"Oh! Because it's full of all kinds of real-life unsolved mysteries. And there's this one mystery I really like, cause, well, okay," she chuckled, "When I was younger, my family always went to this one lake, Yellow Leaf Lake," my stomach unexpectedly twisted as I heard that name. I hadn't been there, heard of it, or even acknowledged its existence for years, and I didn't want to. "Anyway, some girl was murdered there in one of the cabins by the beach. And, I mean, like, brutally murdered. Strangled, stabbed, drowned, all that and more. Then the murderer just dumped her body in the lake and disappeared. No one knows where they went, or even who they were. It's a whole mystery."

"Hundreds of cases go unsolved. That doesn't sound like a murder unique enough to go into a book."

"No, no! The best part is that the killer left evidence everywhere. Fingerprints, hair, even blood. But they still couldn't identify the killer, even with all that. It's like they never existed."

I held my breath. I didn't want to let my nervousness show, but I hated the thought of that dumb murder. I just wanted it to be erased from history.

"What do you think happened? You're the detective."

I took a strong breath and shrugged as if I didn't know. "The murderer was probably some homeless person with an untreated psychotic illness who skipped town and ended their own life after killing the girl."

"That's... oddly specific..."

"Well, *excuse* me. You're the one who wanted my opinion."

"'Cause I thought you'd come up with a good theory, like, it was a ghost or a vampire who everyone thinks died a hundred years ago."

I looked at her in disbelief. I could not, for the life of me, understand what the hell she was going on about. I couldn't even figure out if she was joking or if she was genuinely delusional.

"That's a weirdly specific answer, though. How'd you come up with that?"

I glanced at her but said nothing. She asked again as if I didn't hear her the first time. Again, I said nothing. She furrowed her brows but stopped nagging.

Then there was beautiful, beautiful silence.

"What's your family like?" She pried.

Never mind.

"Excuse me?" My head barely turned to her, my lips as straight as a line with one eyebrow raised.

"Like, your mom and dad and siblings. What are they like?"

"I don't have siblings, and my parents are divorced."

"Oh, that sucks." Harriet slid down in her seat, bored again.

'Please don't ask any more questions, please don't ask any more questions, please don't ask any more questions…'

"But what are your parents like?"

I groaned and was oh so tempted to bang my head on the steering wheel.

"Why do you ask so many questions?"

"I ask questions when I'm curious. Why won't you give me an answer?"

"I don't owe you any personal information."

"But you expect others to answer your questions?"

"Because I ask questions in an investigative manner. I ask questions to obtain information that's valuable to my cases. What you're doing is just petty small-talk."

"You don't get out often, do you?"

My glare turned to ice as I glanced between her and the road.

"That's what I thought. So, what are your parents like?'

"Could we… perhaps just… drive in silence for a while? Like we were doing before?" My

lip began to hurt from my teeth biting down on it after I asked, hoping she would conform to my wishes.

"No. I will literally not stop bugging you until you answer me. Your family has gotta be cool if they raised you."

I groaned in defeat, which was positively music to her ears.

"My family isn't cool, I can promise you that. My parents are divorced, my mom is normal, my dad is wealthy and basically tried to spoil me when I was younger so I'd like him more than my mom."

"Oof..."

"Yeah - oof. Both of my parents are remarried to complete jackasses. My stepmother called me "the embodiment of a nuisance", and my stepfather is just a horrible person whose favorite form of communication was throwing things at your head to get your attention. It's not cool, it just sucks."

Remember how I said I loved silence? Well, I got what I wanted after I said that. I just didn't want it anymore. I glanced at her with a skeptical eye, but all I saw was pity.

"... K... I'm so sorry—"

I interrupted. "Please stop. I hate apologies."

"But, I—"

"Stop."

"... My parents are... sort of the same... Not really. They're still together. But they're pretty wealthy from their dumb business, so we've always been kinda spoiled, I guess..."

"... But?"

"But what?"

"There's always a 'but'."

Recalling some memories that she clearly didn't like, she heavily sighed.

"They do everything they can to make it look like they care, but they really don't. They didn't even notice their son was missing! He handed them a fake permission slip and they signed it without a second thought! They haven't taken those stupid decorations down since they got their first skating rink! What if we want to use the yard, huh? For sports practice or something? But no. We aren't allowed. Because then we'd have to take down all the decorations. It's not like that's a

normal thing or anything, to take down your holiday decorations when Christmas is over!

"But no, they'll just keep them up and embarrass their children who have enough trouble fitting in already! And their great little daughter over here! She's so sweet but, yeah! They'll belittle her until she becomes self-conscious and turns into a bully, pushing people away, including her brother, the only person that genuinely cares about her! And then sure, he can go missing and they won't notice!"

It took me a moment to take in everything. I had never met someone so young who knew exactly what was wrong with them.

"... That... That's very... self-aware."

She sighed and looked out her window, avoiding my gaze. "I had an epiphany recently and I realized I don't really like the person I am." She said plainly, but I could hear a huge amount of pain in her words.

"Oh... Well, that's—"

"You don't have to give me some great metaphor like some wise sage or something," oh, thank Her, "I just realized I don't like myself a few months ago and I haven't really talked to anyone about it, so that was sort of a vent. Sorry."

"No, no, it's fine... It's good to... vent. It's healthy for humans—I mean, for people to express their emotions."

"... Why don't you?"

"What?"

"You barely express emotions. If you do, they're negative."

"... I suppose emotions just aren't that important to me. Besides, even if it's not wise, many people associate emotions with weakness. If you're weak, adults don't take you seriously. Especially if you're young."

"Yeah, well, adults don't know anything. They're just power-hungry kids who pretend they know what they're doing."

My lips curved into a smile, and I laughed. "You're not wrong."

She looked at me with the sweetest grin, so glad she made me laugh.

I smiled back at her, but it faded the smallest bit. "But in all seriousness, it's really mature

of you to realize your mistakes in life and try and fix them."

"Oh, you don't have to be all cheesy..."

"I'm not being cheesy! It's a genuine compliment."

"Oh, well... thank you then." Her cheeks grew rosy, like a beautiful garden blooming in spring.

I felt my cheeks heat as well, watching her smile.

"You're welcome."

Chapter 4

The Marie Enn Motel was a very small, shabby establishment, in size and in service, but it held most of the answers I needed. Though my gut didn't trust it in the slightest, I went in anyway.

I told Harriet to stay in the car while I went in to do my job, but she's Harriet, so of course, she didn't listen. She and I entered through the glass doors and made a beeline for the front desk. No one was present, except for a little bell at the very front with a note that said, "Please Ring". Harriet immediately smashed her hand down on it like a toddler with a one-track mind.

A small woman hobbled out from the back and sat down at the desk, resting her cane on the chair's arm.

"Hello, ladies." She spoke meekly, looking up at us and smiling, her large lips stretching her whole face and all her wrinkles. "How may I help you today?" Her hands trembled as she set them on the computer's keyboard.

I reached into my wallet and retrieved one of my business cards, handing it to her. "Yes, hello, Ma'am. My name is K McIntyre, I'm a

private detective. I'm looking into the case of a missing boy named Abe Hanks. He and another boy,

Nico Ruiz were staying here in this motel for a weekend. I'd like to question your staff on what they've seen, it could be vital to the case."

"Oh... How many rooms would you like again?"

"No, Ma'am, I," I sighed. "Is there anyone else I could speak to?"

Harriet hit my arm. "K! Don't be rude!"

"I'm not being rude! I just asked if there was anyone else I could talk to!"

A girl wearing a room service uniform, carrying a laundry basket full of sheets, passed by, eyeing both me and Harriet. She stopped right behind us.

"You guys are here about that purple haired kid, right? The one that got into a fight with his boyfriend?"

"Yeah!" Harriet eagerly nodded her head. "How'd you know?"

"His boyfriend calls in every once in a while, always asking if "Abe" has come back yet. So, you're a private detective?"

I nodded. "I am. You seem to know a little bit more about what's going on here," I briefly glanced at the ancient being behind the front desk, "would you mind if I questioned you about the case?"

"No, not at all. Question away. Here, we can go to the break room." She led us down a hall to a blue door labeled "Employees Only" and pushed it open. On the other side was a plain looking, grey room with a sofa, a table, a fridge, and other break-room necessities. The three of us took a seat at the rickety table and I once again pulled out my note pad.

"Let's start with your name."

"Oh, uh, Shayla."

"So, Shayla, what do you know about Nico Ruiz and Abe Hanks?"

"I know they came here for some kind of couple get-away - even though this is a bad spot for a couple's getaway - but the black-haired kid totally just, like, left. Grabbed his crap and took a cab home."

"... Do you know why?"

She shook her head. "Not really."

"Did you hear anything like a fight? Yelling, or screaming, anything of the sort?"

"No, not at all."

"Okay... What time did Nico leave?"

"Oh, probably around... 10 am? On Sunday."

I checked back to Nico's notes where he said they started fighting in the early afternoon.

"... Interesting... What happened to Abe after Nico left?"

"Um... A few hours later, he came to the front and waited for, like, twenty minutes, for a cab. He had all his stuff with him."

"And?"

"Well, the cab came and picked him up. I don't know about anything else."

"Do you have security cameras outside the building? Is it possible that they could have picked up the taxi's license plate?"

"I'm really not sure... They're kind of old. And crappy. But I can check if you'd like?"

"I'd sincerely appreciate that."

She nodded. "Okay, I'll be right back." Her chair scraped against the linoleum floor as she got up.

I immediately flipped to a new page and wrote down the huge difference between times. Harriet peered over my notes, curious as she always was.

"Oh, yeah... Nico said he left at, like, 3 in the afternoon. What do you think it means?"

"I'm unsure, but someone's story is inconsistent."

"... What do you think happened to my brother?"

"My best educated guess is that he ran away after the fight to spite Nico or to isolate himself. It is a possibility that something could have happened to him on his way home, but I'm sure he's fine."

"But how do you know? What if he was kidnapped?"

"Your family is rather wealthy, so it's not impossible, but you haven't received a ransom note of any kind yet." I turned an watched her. "Unless you have...?"

She quickly shook her head, urgently extinguishing that thought from my mind.

"Then I'm sure he's perfectly fine."

"But you can't be sure."

I gave her a skeptical eye. "Of *course* I can't be sure. Not until we find him. But every missing person case I've been on, I've found the person."

Mind you, I've only been on one missing person case.

"Really? Every single one?"

"... Yes. Even if it was just a body."

"You—" Her eyes widened greatly, and she slapped her hands down on the table. "You found *BODIES*?!"

"Lower your voice. It was just one."

"That's still a lot of dead people!"

"... You understand that almost a 110 people die every minute, correct?"

"Okay, but to actually *find* a body? You never mentioned this on your blog..."

"... No, it was a rather personal matter, so it wouldn't have been suitable to put on a blog. I was looking for this girl, Valerie Likin, and all my clues led me to a small patch of woods. There were rumors it was cursed, or haunted. No one wanted to go into it to find her. I didn't believe such rumors, and I figured I would find her lost and alone or something of the sort, but... Um..."

"What? Was she murdered?"

"No, she wasn't murdered... Not long after, I found her hanging by a tree."

"...It was suicide...?"

"Yes."

"What—K, that's horrible! You're still so young and you saw something like that?! It would scar me for life. God... How many years ago was that?"

"Um... it was a while ago."

"So, you weren't even eighteen when it happened!"

Oh, trust me, I was **much** *older than eighteen when it happened.*

I simply nodded, and she put her hand on my shoulder.

"Oh, K, that's so horrible..."

"It is. It's a tragedy, really. An innocent person like that, just... gone."

"Yeah..."

"I thought you liked dark things?"

"What? No, I love mysteries. Dark things are cool, but they make me super depressed, so I try and stay away from them. But mysteries are questions with unsolved answers, like puzzles. Some of them are dark, though, but that can't be helped."

"...I suppose you're correct."

"And I know I am." She grinned, but it quickly faded. "So, how old was the girl...?"

I cleared my throat as Shayla came back. She sat back in her chair and slid a piece of paper across the table.

"That's the license plate and name of the cab company. That should help, right?"

I grabbed the paper to confirm this and nodded my head. I let Harriet see as well, of course, because she was already hovering above my shoulder. "Yes, very much so. I appreciate it."

She nodded. "Is there anything else?"

"No," I got up, "there isn't. Thank you for your time."

"Oh, alright."

Harriet awkwardly got up after me, and Shayla led us out of the break room. When we got back to the front, we were very surprised to find Nico sitting in one of the chairs near the door. He was changed out of his gym clothes and had a long, black coat with a bright red scarf.

"Oh, hey guys." He smiled at us and got up. "I didn't know you guys were going to head here right away."

"We had no reason not to."

"Yeah, I know, I just… I don't know. Anyway."

"How and why are you here? During the interrogation, you said you didn't have a car."

"Oh, I took a cab, and I forgot a bracelet here after the fight, so I just wanted to come back and get it. It's kind of important to me."

"Is it black? With a silver buckle?" Shayla quizzed from behind us.

"Yeah! It is! Do you know where it is?"

"Yeah, it's in the lost and found. I'll go get it for you."

"Thank you again for your time, Shayla." I thanked her before she walked away. She simply nodded and wandered off. "Let's go, Harriet." I passed Nico, seeming to ignore his existence before he stopped me.

"Hey, do you think I could get a ride home…? My cab left already."

I stopped dead in my tracks and swirled around to him, flat face and pale eyes. "It only would have left if you paid the driver, so why did you already pay?"

"I… What?"

"The cab only would have left if you paid it. If you knew you were going to need a ride home, why did you pay it?" I took a step closer and he took one back, just in time, like a puppet and its master.

"K! God, let's just give him a ride." Harriet interrupted on the moment and pretended to act annoyed, but the masked look I saw on her face whispered to me that she was worried. Once she realized I was analyzing her, she rolled her eyes. "Whatever."

I briefly looked at Nico. "We'll be waiting for you in my car," I announced to him coldly. "Don't be long."

I saw him nod, then I turned back and continued on my path. Harriet locked arms with me as we left the building.

"Why are you acting so suspicious of him?" She questioned, a skeptical look on her face.

"I don't trust him," I stated simply, but I knew that wouldn't suffice. Not for her. So, I added, "I think he kidnapped Abe."

Her eyes widened, but she said nothing, to both her and my surprise.

My eyes led my head as I glanced back at the building. I had a gut feeling, and my gut didn't like that building. My gut had some sort of vendetta against it, which is rather odd since it's a gut. "Give me a moment." I detached myself from Harriet and stood by

the glass windows next to the entrance, sneakily peering inside.

Watching into the windows, I saw Shayla come back and give Nico something small, probably the bracelet. But Nico reached into his pocket and pulled out a wad of cash, handing it to Shayla.

I knew it. I don't know what I knew, but I knew it.

Harriet was staring at me, justly confused. I ran back over to her and ushered her hastily towards the car. "Get in, get in, get in!"

"Okay, okay, okay!"

She entered the car quickly on her side, and I entered mine.

"Act natural."

"No one ever says that with good intentions."

"Shhh!"

Nico walked by the car a few seconds later, so Harriet opened and stuck her head out of her window to get his attention. "Hey! We're in this one."

He got into the backseat and grinned sweetly at us. "I got my bracelet!" He held up his

wrist, exposing a black leather bracelet with a silver clip.

"I see."

The car purred as it started up, but I groaned when I saw the fuel gauge.

"We need gas."

I stopped by the nearest gas station and filled up my tank, but when I got back in the car, Harriet was faced as far away from Nico as she possibly could be. Her expression seemed mildly angry and confused, but mostly sad.

I looked between her and Nico, who was also avoiding eye contact.

"... Okay... Did something happen?" I asked Harriet, who looked at me with her eyebrows raised.

"No, why?"

"You're both seated away from each other as though you're siblings fighting over who gets the family fortune now that your father has died of polio, and one of you just brought up the wishes of your mother who said you two should share the fortune, but she was tragically murdered several years ago so it's a sensitive topic."

Harriet stared at me, comically perplexed. "What the hell? Who are you, Shakespeare?"

I shrugged. "In another life."

Nico subtly put a hand over his mouth, trying to hold in a chuckle, which was suspicious. My jokes aren't funny unless you're me, so why did he laugh?

Ignoring all my suspicions, I got in and started the car, heading back to the city.

Nico and Harriet spent most of the ride having all kinds of friendly conversations, recalling anecdotes, and laughing.

"Do you," Harriet stopped, giggling like a maniac, "Do you remember when Mrs. Chapner dropped her bag, and everything spilled out, and a random burger just came rolling out?"

Nico cackled. "OH, MY GOD, YES!"

I tuned out most of their conversations, but I'm glad I was eavesdropping for this one. It seemed perfectly normal, both laughing, commenting on some kind of burger. Then, Harriet turned towards Nico, about to continue, when she said, "Roman, do you remember when..."

My parasympathetic nervous system kicked in unannounced as soon as I heard that name. I panicked, to say the least, and slammed the brake to the floor. The car screeched to a halt on the empty highway.

Chapter 5

Harriet almost slammed forward at the sudden stop. She whipped around to face me. "What the hell?!"

I kept a tight grip on the steering wheel to keep my hands from shaking, but it did not work precisely as I hoped, because the steering wheel started shaking. I quickly took my hands off the wheel and folded them tightly in my lap, then looked at Harriet.

"You called him the wrong name."

"What? Oh!" Her eyes widened. "Oh."

"His name isn't Roman." I looked back at Nico, who just seemed wildly confused. "You aren't Roman."

He raised his hands in defense "It's just a nickname…!"

"A nickname from *what*?"

"The school play in ninth grade! We did a modern version of Romeo and Juliet, and I played the Romeo character named Roman!"

My stare turned cold as ice. There was my gut once again, twisting and turning, screaming at me to kick him out of the car. I didn't, because

I didn't know whom to trust. Nico, some kid I had just met, or my gut? My heart pounded loudly as it pumped adrenaline through my veins, but despite this, I could barely move a muscle.

The only one I knew I trusted was Harriet. She didn't seem it, but she was wise. She wouldn't lie to me, would she? I looked at her with pleading eyes to tell me the honest truth. Her eyebrows raised, and she gulped nervously.

She gently nodded her head, "He's telling the truth."

I almost wanted it to be a lie. I wanted him to be Roman. And I hated that, so I retreated back into my seat and began driving again.

The rest of the drive was quiet. It was suffocating. But, instead of swimming for air, I let myself choke.

We dropped Nico off at his home, then headed back to my apartment. I hadn't said anything in quite some time, and it looked like Harriet was concerned.

"K... I just—"

I stopped her.

"13."

"What?"

"Valerie. The girl I found hanging by the tree. She was 13... You asked earlier."

"Right. Yeah…that's… horrible. It must have been hard finding her."

My head slightly tilted forward for a nod, remembering the grieving faces of her family when they were told, and their outrage when they found out it was suicide. It was something I thought I would be ready for, but I wasn't. The image still made my stomach twist, my mind cloud, and my heart ache.

"It's part of being a detective." I spouted as though it was common knowledge, knowing how full of crap I was, just trying to push my emotions back down and get rid of this empty feeling in my chest.

Getting back to my apartment, we headed inside immediately to avoid the cold. It was already dark, and Harriet complained about being hungry, so I made us a meal.

"Why do you only have, like, three forks?" She questioned, snooping around my kitchen.

"Because I always clean my dishes and I never have anyone over," I said as I put chicken

breasts into the oven and put a pot of pasta on the stove.

"Not even like a significant other or something?"

I shook my head. “People don’t really like me that much. They say I’m arrogant.”

“Because you are.”

“Correct, but I’m also adorable.” I grinned at her, to which she rolled her eyes with a matching smile.

We had supper once it was done, and I put cleaning off for now so we could get straight to work. I pulled a large corkboard out and began pinning notes and pictures up to it.

Harriet ran her hand gently along the side of it. “Is that corkboard thing detectives do really necessary?”

“Not really, but it’s cool.”

“Nice. So… Do you still think Nico did it…?”

A sigh pushed past my lips as I solemnly nodded. “He acts like a perfectly normal person, but he seems possessive and manipulative.”

“I just… How do you know?”

“… If I answered that, you’d laugh at me.”

“Probably but now you have to answer anyway.”

I groaned. How was this girl my main source of annoyance and amusement all at the same time?

"My gut sort of… tells me things. And not in the normal way, like you get a bad feeling if something is wrong. It genuinely talks to me, and it told me not to trust him."

"… That's—"

"The dumbest thing you've ever heard?"

"Yeah." We said in unison, then she laughed.

"Okay, that sounds super dumb, but like, I get it. Sort of. And you've solved all those cases so far, so, I trust you." She beamed.

"Well, it isn't just a gut feeling. He also gave money to that girl we spoke to who works at Marie Enn, Shayla, when he went to "get his bracelet"."

"And you didn't question him about it after? Why not?"

"Gut. I'm also sure he has a motive. He seems irritated about Abe not being out, and Shayla didn't know anything about a fight. That motel is small, and the walls are clearly thin. If there's was a fight as big as Nico suggested it was, everyone in that building would have heard it."

She shrugged. "I guess… What's next?"

"I want to call the cab company and ask where they dropped off Abe."

"Cool. What can I do?"

I handed her a small box. "Take these pins and string and draw random red lines between all the pictures on the corkboard. Pretend you're in a detective movie trying to solve a huge case."

"Can you play epic detective music in the background?"

"No, but you can listen to it on your phone with headphones."

"Hell yeah." She cracked a big smile and immediately pulled her earbuds out of her bag as I referenced the piece of paper given to me earlier for the cab company's name. I researched them, then called the number on their website.

It took quite some time to deal with them, as they said they had to keep customer confidentiality, which I know is BS, but eventually, they gave me the number of the man who drives the car with the license plate Shayla gave me.

I thought it would be much easier dealing with the actual person. It wasn't.

"No, sir, this isn't a prank caller, I," I groaned. "I am a private investigator, I just need to ask you a few questions—"

Click.

"Sir? Sir, are you there? He hung up on me."

"How rude." Harriet chuckled, so I told her to shut up.

She finished playing with pins and string ages ago, so at the moment she was simply on her phone, looking at whatever memes teenagers look at.

I tried calling again but he didn't pick up.

"Hey, K?"

"Yeah?"

"Why did you lie?"

"What on earth do you mean?"

"About the girl. Valerie Likin. You said you found her."

"...You looked her up?"

"Yeah. It says some policeman name Aaron DeGagne found her thirty years ago. Why did you lie?"

I didn't answer. I had one, but it wasn't one I was willing to tell her.

"Okay, why the hell do you always do that? You never answer my questions."

"Sometimes there are questions that shouldn't be answered, and sometimes there are answers that shouldn't be questioned."

"Wha… What?"

I smiled, knowing Plan: Spout Some Random BS And Hope It Confuses Her Enough to Stop Asking Questions was a success.

"Why are you so weird?" She asked, deadpan look.

Plan: Spout Some Random BS And Hope It Confuses Her Enough to Stop Asking Questions was a sort of a success.

"Because I'm not a normal person."

She rolled her eyes, looking back to the art she created on the corkboard. "Ain't that the truth. What's next, since cab dude won't talk to you?"

"Well, I want to investigate Nico further. I'll take you to school in the morning, then I need you to stay there to let me in when I get there in the late afternoon. Hopefully, all students will be gone by then. I want to check Abe and Nico's lockers, and with luck, we'll find something useful. We should get rest for now. It's late."

"Whaaatt? It's only, like, eight o'clock."

"It's 11:30."

"Oh, real shit? Okay, fair enough."

I got up from my chair. "Come on, I'll drive you home."

"What? Nooo, let me stay here for the night. Please? That way it'll take less time to get to the school if you don't have to pick me up and take me with you!"

"I would expect you to get to school on your own."

"PLEEEEEAASSSEEEEEEE?" She begged loudly and annoyingly, starting to give me a headache.

"Freaking—FINE. If you're staying here, call your parents first."

She shrugged. "They won't care."

I took her phone out of her hands, then went into the contacts and called her mom. I handed back the phone as it began ringing. "Make them care."

Harriet took the couch. I set her up with most of my blankets and pillows so she wouldn't get cold, and she seemed to sleep peacefully throughout the night.

When morning finally did come, I was up and I completed my morning routine far before Harriet was awake. I was going to wait until Harriet was awake to make breakfast, so for now, I had nothing to do. So, I decided to torture myself with guilt, fear, and regret.

I opened my laptop and searched "Yellow Leaf Lake murder".

There were hundreds upon hundreds of results, and I read as many as I could. So many of them held misinformation, and some of them were just theories about what happened, but no matter how much pain reading each word in each article brought me, I continued. It was like drowning again, but I was drowning myself. I had the opportunity to swim up for air and survive, but I continued to swim deeper.

Until I was forcefully pulled up.

"Reading about Yellow Leaf Lake murder?" Harriet asked, her head appearing beside mine.

I yelled, "NOTHING!" And quickly shut my computer.

She gave me a look as though I had two heads. "Freaking weirdo. You're acting like I caught you watching porn or something."

I rolled my eyes at her crudeness and opened my computer again. She wrapped her arms around my neck from behind, placing her head on top of mine.

"... What are you doing?"

"Hugging you."

"Why?"

"Because hugging is something friends do."

"… Okay. Anyway, you simply had me intrigued from yesterday."

"Cool. Why are you crying?"

"What? I'm not crying." I put a hand to my cheek and felt the wetness of a salty tear running down my pale skin. "Oh… Um. You can go have a shower if you'd like one. I'll start making breakfast."

"Wait, K…"

She kept me from getting up, gently pushing me back into my seat.

"… Yes?"

"Can I ask a question?"

"I suppose."

"Who is Roman?"

Hearing her ask that was painful and left a strange void in my chest as if she reached her hand through my skin so she could violently rip out my heart.

Why, of all things, did she have to ask that? Why about Roman? As if I didn't think about Roman enough.

"Roman is… No one."

"Are you sure...? Because you seemed really worked up yesterday... It was a lot of emotion for "no one"." Moving to the side, she let go of me and looked down at me, but I looked away.

I sighed. "Roman isn't no one... Roman is someone from a part of my past that I'm not proud of. Someone I'd hate to run into nowadays. But Roman's dead, so there's no need to worry."

"Oh, I'm so sorry..."

"Sorry? For who? For me? Don't be. I'm glad that Roman is dead." I stood up, facing away from her.

"Then I'm sorry you hated them so much you couldn't even mourn."

It felt like my heart stopped—like everything stopped. The unwelcome pain in my chest strangled and ceased my ability to respond as her words easily slipped out of her mouth. She could walk away without a care in the world, but even hours later I felt myself going back to the conversation. It played over and over and over in my head like a broken record that didn't want to be fixed.

Chapter 6

My car slid slightly on the icy road as I rounded the corner into the school parking lot. Parking was easy since the lot was barren under the light of the moon. Harriet and I ended up waiting until nightfall to make sure there were less possible witnesses. Technically, what we were doing wasn't illegal. But it was much easier doing matters like this secretly, so I wasn't constantly being questioned whether or not I should be doing them in the first place.

I waited at the door Harriet and I planned. When she let me in, I slowly closed it behind me, ensuring not even the squeak of rusty screws was heard.

"What locker is his?" I inquired quietly, quickly checking down each hallway.

"309. I don't know the combination, though." She whispered in response.

"We'll figure it out. Were you spotted? Does anyone know you're still here?"

"No, I hid in an unused classroom until everyone left."

"Excellent."

We tiptoed down each hallway, careful to examine it before carrying on our way. Our quest to Nico's locker was uninterrupted by any remaining students, staff, or janitors. The ghost town of a school was stiller than the night itself and almost as dark.

Dark blue lockers with colorful locks paved the way to Nico's locker, near the middle of the empty hall. The link keeping locker 309 closed was large, bulky and rectangular. It had 12 small buttons, a number from 1-12 next to each button.

"This is a… peculiar lock."

Harriet nodded, leaning against Nico's neighboring locker. "He had it custom made. It's a 4-number combination."

"Alright, well, you know him much better than I do. You should try first."

I stepped out of the way, letting Harriet try as many combinations as her mind could collect.

"Maybe it was… 4-7-12-6…? Nope." She groaned, her seventh attempt not working.

"If it wasn't a four-number combination I'd suggest 1-2-5, the numeric version of Abe."

She shined her phone's flashlight at the lock again thoughtfully. "Well… Maybe it's another word? Can you think of anything?"

My stomach twisted, and all I could think was 'Yes.' But I couldn't say it.

"No. You know him much better. Do you have an idea?"

"No, not really."

While she continued trying random numbers, I had a war inside my head. My fear and my apathy battled for the right over my mind, my fear spouting everything that could go wrong, while my apathy destroyed every argument. And all I could do was stand there and wonder which would win.

Without too much effort, my apathy reigned victorious.

"Hey, Harriet? Can I give it a try?"

"Um… Yeah, I suppose so. You have an idea?"

"Yes, but it probably won't work."

"Well, it's worth a shot!" She stepped back, out of the way.

I took a deep breath, sounding more nervous than anyone should have been in this scenario. I watched Harriet from the corner of my eye for a null moment. Despite noticing my nervousness, she simply gave a small, reassuring smile, and said nothing.

Before I approached Nico's locker, I turned fully to her. "Hey, why don't you see what you can find in Abe's locker? See if you can find anything useful to the case. You know his combination, don't you?"

She looked off thoughtfully, slowly nodding. "Yeah… I think so… Yeah. Okay, I'll go check his locker. Be right back!" She smiled and ran off, but something about her smile was… forced. Fake. It unsettled me. However, I was immediately distracted when I turned back to Nico's locker. The darkness Harriet left as she went to go check Abe's locker was haunting, and the locker didn't help.

I felt as though that locker held both the destruction and savior of the universe at the same time. But what was it that Roman always used to say? If you worry, you suffer twice? Roman was always so much more carefree than I was. They couldn't care less about people. Unless that person was me. Then they couldn't care more.

My head kept telling me I was out of my mind, but still, I listened. My fear was revived from battle and it was out for revenge, making my legs step backward unconsciously, as if they were aware of some calamity about to occur.

The metal of the locker and locker lightly clanked together as I put my tremoring fingers against the buttons, using my other hand to hold my phone for light.

I spelled out the word in my head, then used the alphabet to match the letters to their numerical counterparts.

L. 12.

I wasn't really sure why I was trying it.

A. 1.

Even if I was scared, I convinced myself it wouldn't work.

K. 11.

It was just a waste of time.

E. 5.

Click.

Before, my stomach felt like a brick in a washing machine. Now, the twisting was gone. So was everything else. In its place was a hole. A big, black hole filled with nothing but black and void.

The lock hung limply from the locker's handle. My whimpering hand reached for it and took it off, then carefully opened the small, metal door.

Among the contents of the locker, only one thing stood out. My hand reached forward and squeezed past many educational textbooks to reach a box at the very back. Despite the box's small sized, I struggled to pick it up. Wondering what was so heavy that it took quite some strength to carry, I tore it open.

There were three books filled to the brim with creepy sketches of people and rotting bodies. They made my skin crawl and give me shivers so bad I felt cold with two jackets on. I shoved them aside, happy to start forgetting what I had just seen. I soon realized what made the box so heavy, other than the books. There were maybe 10 bottles of cheap paint, paint brushes, and an assortment of dark nail polishes. One color I recognized from Harriet's nails.

The last thing was something I gladly pushed off. The bright yellow border surrounding the thin, folded up paper turned my interest away. But since I was here to find anything suspicious that I could, I flipped it over to see what it was.

The hole in my stomach created a cold, empty feeling I tried to ignore, but no matter how much I tried to, I really couldn't. It was too painful. The feeling only got worse when I read the title of the small pamphlet.

WELCOME TO YELLOW LEAF LAKE!

My mind rushing to find answers, I quickly unfolded it. The map was a vacation directory, showing off all the vendors and cabins near the lake. One cabin, in particular, was circled in big, black marker.

My ears starting ringing so loudly that I didn't even hear the tip-tap of shoes nearing me. The rapid footsteps rounded the corner, but I was sure it was Harriet, so I didn't turn to see who it was. I calmly placed the pamphlet back in the box, then turned. At first, all I saw was the barrel of a gun.

Stepping back, I looked up at the wielder of the weapon and saw Nico's grinning face.

"Right on schedule." He cocked his head gently to the side, holding his stance.

I felt almost completely paralyzed. The part of my mind that wouldn't let me believe Nico was who I thought he was, *finally* died as he and I stared, thousands of words being exchanged through simple, excruciating eye contact.

"All of your hard work at Yellow Leaf Lake, all put to waste, huh?" He taunted, a smirk plastered on his face from ear to ear.

"So, you did fake it…"

"Of course I faked it! Do you think I'm an idiot?! The only thing that kept me going was the thought of seeing the look on your face right now." He chuckled darkly, his eyebrows narrowing.

"How did you get into the school? The doors are locked."

His smirk simply grew. "I hid with Harriet. She's been working with me this whole time."

"What… No, she hasn't! You're lying!"

He scoffed, placing his free hand on his hip. "You're just angry you didn't figure it out."

I growled lowly, trying not to let any other emotions escape. "Roman, you need to stop this. It's one thing to hurt me, but you're involving innocent people in this now."

He laughed, "Oh, but when you involved innocent people, it was fine! You're as selfish as ever, Lake. You never change. And you were the love of my existence! But how did you repay me? With DAYS of TORTURE!"

"Roman, you were out of control! You stalked me constantly and destroyed things and relationships I cherished. If anyone hasn't changed, it's you."

He steadied his gun, realizing he'd let it slouch, then carefully aimed for me. "Don't you dare— "

"Don't shoot!" Harriet suddenly stepped in front of me, her arms out and eyes closed out of fear, ready to take the bullet.

"HARRIET, NO!" I held my breath, unable to move, but I never heard the gunshot.

"Harriet. Get out of the way, now." Roman demanded, keeping his aim.

"No. I'm done playing your game. I'm not letting you hurt her, and I want my damn

brother back. I'm done 'working for you', and lying to K."

"Harriet, if you ever want to see Abe again, you'll—"

"If YOU ever want to see him again, then you better start running! We called the police on the way here, and they're already headed to Yellow Leaf Lake." She lied. "They're going to take Abe away and arrest you, and you'll never see him ever again."

My immediate thought was about how stupid that sounded. He wouldn't care.

But when I looked back at Roman, he was terrified. He met my eyes for a moment as he started to back away, tucking his gun into his belt. He hastily turned and ran.

I realized, when he left, that I had been holding my breath. I gasped for air, clutching my stomach.

"Oh, my lord…" I leaned against the lockers, my panicked heart feeling as though it were to explode with how fast it was beating.

It seemed like Harriet was feeling the same because she crippled over onto her knees.

"Ooohhh holy mother of - Mmmmmmy god I did not think that was going to work."

"You… didn't? Why on earth would you act on a plan that you didn't think was going to work?!"

"I don't know. Spite, and probably dumbness, I guess."

I leaned my head back and let out a laugh. "You… Teenagers… They're so dumb…"

"Yeah, yeah. Insult me later. We can't relax now, we need to panic some more! Come on, Roman is probably headed to the beach house already. We need to beat him there!"

I nod and stood up straight, "You're right, and I'll explain everything on the way there."

"Oh, thank god." She sighed in relief, as if asking me questions was going to be hell. Grabbing her hand as I ran by her, we quickly raced back to the car.

Chapter 7

"So, how did you know Abe was at Yellow Leaf Lake? Did you know all along?" I buckled my seatbelt, then gave her a quizzical look as I started the engine.

She clicked her seatbelt into place and shook her head. "No, I found a pamphlet in Abe's locker that had one of the directory things from the lake. One of the cabins was circled, and Abe had written "Go here" next to it."

"Ah."

She bit her lip for a moment, then sighed. "I'll go first with the whole... explaining thing. So, the whole case was a plan to set you up, as I'm sure you've already realized. And I was in on it. It wasn't willingly since I just wanted my brother back and Roman threatened to take him away forever if I didn't comply, but... I'm still so sorry that I lied to you, and lead you on this entire time..."

My teeth bit down on my tongue, keeping myself from telling her off. I was obviously angry with her, but I couldn't say it. I couldn't look her in the eyes and tell her I was upset, because I knew it wasn't her fault.

"It's alright, Harriet. I understand." I forcefully smiled at her. "So, you knew he was safe the whole time?"

"Well, I definitely questioned his safety, but I also knew Roman would never purposefully hurt Abe."

"What's the deal with the two of them? Are they actually dating?"

"Yeah. They started dating three years ago in ninth grade, but Abe and I have known Roman since middle school. We were that one inseparable group of friends. We always knew there was something weird about Roman, we just… didn't know what. His real name is Nico, but he insists on everyone calling him Roman. Until about two months ago, that is, in preparation for his plan. And he always talked about someone named Lake… I guess that's you, huh?"

"So, you know what we are? Roman and I?"

"What? No, not at all. Roman never explained "what you are". He always said weird things, like he knew too much. Then, when we questioned him about it, he wouldn't answer. Huh. Sounds like someone else I know." She grinned playfully.

I rolled my eyes, my lips curving into a small smile. "Yes, I suppose people like me do that often, but it's for good reason. It's hard to explain to humans, and often they don't believe us. If they do, they ask ludicrous questions."

"... So, you gonna actually tell me what the hell you are, or are you just going to be edgy."

"I was planning on just being edgy."

She groaned, so I let a small laugh escape from my smiling face.

"I'm kidding. I'll tell you."

"Good, because you promised to and I'd be really mad if you broke it. So, what are you?"

I took a deep breath, gathering all my strength to try and explain this. I still had fears from all the other times I told mortals and they reacted in unpredicted and usually violent ways.

"... Do you know what reincarnation is?"

She took a moment to take in my small sentence, her eyes widening significantly. "Wait... WAIT. Wait, hold on. Okay. So... You... You and Roman... Like, reincarnate? Like, the die and come back thing?"

"Yeah."

"Okay, okay, okay, wait. So. Every time you die... you come back? Is this like a Groundhog Day situation, or, like, you're stuck in a video game?" She gasped. "Are we in a video game?!"

"No, Harriet, we're not in a video game. And it's not like Groundhog Day, either. Every time I die, I'm born as a new person. The person isn't usually random. I've noticed that I'm always born in the same area as where I died, near the closest person giving birth."

"You're a different person every lifetime...?"

"Precisely. I regain all of my memories about a month after being born and grow up all over again."

"So, you have a new family every time too... Do you get along with them every time?"

"I try my best not to associate with the family I have. I prefer being alone, so I usually spend most of my time in whatever room they provide me with. It just makes it easier when I'm old enough to leave, so they don't have any attachment to me, and I don't have any attachment to them."

"What? Isn't that kind of unfair? I mean, they're going through all the trouble of raising you, and you don't even, like, go back to visit for the holidays or birthdays?"

"No, I don't see the use for it. And trust me, I'm never any kind of burden to raise. Well, other than this lifetime..."

"Were you a trouble-kid?"

"No, I simply rushed this life because I was eager to get back into detective work, and it backfired. I graduated high school at ten, which caused quite the kickback. News coverage, talk of experiments and brain scans, investigations on my family and my school. It was discord, to be frank. I'll be wise to remember not to do that in my next life."

Silence took hold for a moment before Harriet gladly broke its rein. "Wait, hold on, Aaron DeGagne..."

"Was my previous life, yes."

"So, Valerie... it was you that found her..."

"It was one of my darkest days. I knew her before she went missing. She was one of the kindest people I've ever known, so I figured it was only a matter of time."

"What...?"

"Humans often masquerade their feelings. That's not an observation, it's just a fact. I find that humans always express somewhat of the opposite of how they're feeling. She was depressed but acted happily.

You masqueraded as a bully because you were feeling insecure."

"... You should write a book."

"I already have."

"You should write a book about your life."

"I'm sure someone else already has."

"Okay, so why do you hate Roman?"

"I don't hate him."

"You said you were glad he was gone when you thought he was dead."

"So? I'm glad when the snow is gone, it doesn't mean I hate the snow. Roman and I are the same. He's reborn the same way I am, and we were put on earth together. We made a pact to always find each other in the next life and to stick together. In some lifetimes, we were lovers--"

"Ew."

"--and Roman seemed perfectly happy like that. But he started to get too attached like he does to everything. He didn't want us to befriend humans, and when I suggested we travel the planet instead of just staying wherever we were born, he got upset and said I was trying to "escape him". That was the first red flag."

"So, it was an abusive relationship... That doesn't sound like Roman, though! Not to be the devil's advocate, but he's a weirdly selfless person. He was the one that inspired me to change."

"He had a talent for that... Besides, it wasn't abusive. Not physically, anyway. The only times he tried hurting me is when we were out of the relationship."

"You know that doesn't sound any better, right?"

My shoulders rose, tensing up a bit. "It's not that bad for immortal souls. He killed me a few times, I killed him a few times."

"Are there any others? Any other immortals?"

"Plenty. Or, at least, there were. The last time I saw them was when they invited me to join a suicide pact."

"Oookay, what about the name thing? The K, and Nico, and Roman, and Lake whatever. What's all that about?"

"Those are our god names. Lake is mine, Roman is his. I go by K because it's the initial of my birth name, and it's simply easier to go by your initial than completely change your name the way Roman does."

"Wait, so, are you, like, the god of water? And that's why you're called Lake? And Roman is the god… of… Romans?"

"No, not at all. "Lake" and "Roman" are simply what our names sound like. They're in no way connected the English words. They mean something completely different."

"What do they mean?"

"Well, they don't really… mean things. They just are. Roman's name technically 'means' passionate, which makes a lot of sense."

"And Lake?"

"Lake is… really more up to interpretation. It "means" image."

"Image? Like a photo?" She sat back and crossed one leg over the other.

"Not exactly. It's more like, imagination, color, a deeper meaning."

"Wow, that… really is up to interpretation."

"I know. That's why I despise my human name…"

"You could get it legally changed?"

"There's no point really. It's just a waste of money, and humans already insist on making everything progressively more expensive."

"Yikes. True. So, you guys are gods? Why are you on earth?"

I sighed, "Okay, imagine you are a god. The god of gods."

"The supreme god."

"Correct. Imagine you're Her, and you make a new species called "humans". They destroy everything and will eventually begin to actively kill their planet by overindulgence in consumerism."

"Yeah, yeah, humans are horrible, got it."

"But the idea is that they're supposedly good on the inside, and even though lots of them are horrible, there are hundreds trying to

stand up against the bad humans and make a change. Basically, you create a vicious cycle of horrible beings against good beings, just to see what will happen. Now, you speak to the gods under you to ask what they think. They tell you outright that it's a bad idea, because it is. So, what do you do?"

"Accept criticism and feedback, asking where they think I need to improve...?"

"No. You're a god, so you're a dramatic bitch and you over-react to everything."

"Right."

"So, your underlings hate your humans. What do you do to them as eternal torture for what you call 'ignorance and betrayal'?"

She lifted her head slightly, her eyes widening in realization. "… Make them humans."

"Precisely. And not just once, or twice, but over and over and over and over again. You know how you humans believe in a heaven and hell?"

"I mean I was an atheist before this, but sure."

"This is our hell. And the only way to escape it is to kill ourselves."

"But you'd just come back..."

"Well, there is one way for us to die. To wish for nonexistence, then end our mortal bodies." I took a small, shaky breath. "It's what I tried to do to Roman at Yellow Leaf."

"So… You were the murderer… And roman was that woman… That's how you knew what happened."

I nodded. "I'm not saying what I did was right, but I had my reasons. Roman was obsessive, and I couldn't live with him. A few more lives passed before I finally left him, but he kept finding me and trying to force me to come back to him. Eventually, I had to kill him to stop stalking me."

"You killed him first?"

"Well, yes, but—"

"So, you understand you started the cycle of murder?"

"Harriet, a human like you couldn't possibly—"

"Nah, nah, nah, don't disregard what I'm saying just cause I'm not a god like you." I looked at her as if a second head had suddenly sprouted from her neck. "Yeah, that's right. I use the word disregard now.

Roman shouldn't have stalked you the way he did, but you started this... vicious cycle of murder, and now you're caught in it, trying to convince yourself you didn't start it in the first place."

"Harriet... You have no idea the kind of situation it was."

"Yes, I do, because you literally just explained it, and I trust you explained it exactly how it went. He shouldn't have been stalking you, and he definitely has some kind of abandonment issues -- which he should totally go to a therapist about by the way.

Wait, do gods have therapists? Never mind, not important right now… Do they?"

"Harriet."

"Right, yes, save the dumb questions for later. Okay, but you get my point, right? It's like, this guy, Tony, punched me once, so I punched him back. And then I got in trouble, which was super weird! Because, he punched me first, so why should I get in trouble? Well, I found out that earlier that day after I jokingly tripped him in the hallways, he landed on his backpack and broke this clay art piece he worked super hard on in art class. It was supposed to be a present for his mom."

"What does that have to do with me and Roman?"

"Just cause I accidentally broke his clay thing didn't mean it was okay for him to punch me! And it definitely didn't mean I was allowed to punch him back. I shouldn't have tripped him, especially since I saw him put the sculpture into his bag, but two wrongs don't make a right. Roman shouldn't have stalked you, and he should have been a lot more respectful of your wishes, but that doesn't mean it was justified for you to kill him."

She was right. She was way too right, and I didn't want to believe her. Everything would have been so much easier if I had just accepted the truth, but I didn't want to be wrong. After all, I was never wrong.

"Okay, I'll let you think over my amazing therapist skills," she gloated, "but I have one more question."

I quietly waited for her to ask, immaturely wanting to play the silent game.

"Are we alone in the universe?"

"What do you mean?"

"Like, are there other species out there, in space? Or are we completely alone?"

"We're alone."

"What? But you said that your god made humans. So, she didn't make any other species?"

"No, she did."

"Then..."

"She made other species, but they're like us. They're alone too"

Chapter 8

I moved my hands, trying to feel the inside of the lock on the door to the cabin Abe was supposed to be in. I was thankful that I had a lockpicking set still inside my car from my move. Harriet was concerned that I had a lockpicking set in the first place. Harriet shivered as the wind picked up, and she huddled closer to me. "Do you have it yet…?"

"Almost… aaand… there!" The lock clicked, so I put my tools in my pocket. I pulled the door open, and we got a blast of air from the inside so warm that it hurt my eyes. I squinted, and we stepped inside.

Footsteps hasted to the door. "Roman, I thought you weren't— " They stopped. "…Harriet?"

Harriet turned to a purple haired boy now standing by the front closet. He was identical to her, which was no surprise, but *was* slightly unsettling. Her face lit up with so much happiness and relief.

"Abe! You're okay!"

The boy stood up and they ran to each other, embracing immediately. They kept their arms around each other while talking.

"I was so freaking worried… You said you were just going on a friggen trip with Roman… You didn't even tell your sister you were getting fake kidnapped…"

He laughed, holding her tighter. "I knooow… I'm so sorry… I'm okay…"

As they embraced, I looked around the familiar cabin. They changed many things, like the windows, flooring, and wall color. Why wouldn't they? A murder was committed within these walls. I stared at the living room, remembering all the things I did in that room. The smell of blood and sweat, the muffled screaming, the whimpering, and the sight of blood mixing with tears.

I was brought back to the present when Harriet let go of Abe and they separated. She turned to me. "Abe, this is K McIntyre—"

"The person who killed Roman." He narrowed his eyes, his expression changing from joyous and kind to unforgiving and ruthless.

My eyes broadened, my lips remaining straight as a line. "Oh. It appears you're well informed."

"That I am."

"Wait, Abe, you know about Roman?"

He glanced at her, his eyes softening. "That he's a god and always reincarnates? Yeah, obviously. And I know exactly what K did." Turning back to me, he glared once more.

I rolled my eyes at this. "Yes, yes, I'm horrible. We get it. We need to leave, now."

"Come on, Abe. Let's go." Harriet linked her arm in his, but he pushed her back.

"No! I'm staying here until Roman comes back."

I sighed. "Abe, listen, I know you love him but he's currently unstable, and he's armed." Abe's eyes softened again, surprised. "It's unsafe to be here, for anyone. Let's get out of here while we still can."

"It's a little too late for that, Lake."

I pivoted my head to the right and was staring down the same barrel of the same gun from before.

"Oh. Roman. Care to join us?" I asked, sarcasm seething through my teeth.

"Hands up! Don't you dare move!" He growled, then looked at the twins. "Abe, wait for me outside."

Abe grabbed a blanket and started to make his way outside, keeping his head down.

"Harriet, go with your brother." I commanded, to which Roman pressed the gun against my head.

"Shut up!"

"K, no, I'm not leaving! What if he—"

"He won't shoot. Now, go."

She visibly hesitated, then scurried after her brother.

I stepped back, away from Roman, raising my arms to satisfy him. "This has to end, Roman. You know that."

"Do you know how long I've been waiting for this, Lake?" He took a nervous step forward, the gun in his hands trembling. His face was far from nervous, however. It was focused, precise, and calculated. Something he always mocked me for being.

"74 years and 6 months. I've been counting." I announced without hesitation.

He growled lowly, the fire in his eyes only growing brighter. "Counting out the days you thought you were rid of me?"

"Counting out the days I missed you."

"Shut up! It's too late to grovel."

I rolled my eyes. "We both know my ego is far too big to grovel. I missed you, Roman. I did. Hurting you hurt me."

"SHUT UP! JUST SHUT UP!" He momentarily looked down and let out a small sob, clenching his teeth. "I could just kill you, right now. There's nothing stopping me."

"What good would it do anyway? I'll come back, you'll go to prison for murder and never see Abe again."

"I'll miss Abe, but I'll kill myself before they can put me in prison, then I'll find you in the next life and do the same thing… over and over. Find you. Kill you. Die. Find you. Kill you. Die."

"And what will you be accomplishing? Our cycle will only continue. It never stops. It needs to."

"I've made up my mind!" He kept his head down, closing his eyes while he yelled.

"Minds can change, Roman. Please, think about what you're doing."

He was silent, contemplating for a moment, then he raised his gun. A single tear streaked down his cheek. "I have."

He shot.

Chapter 9

I jumped over the stairs of the porch, almost tripping into the snow. I swiftly regained my balance and bolted in between other cabins, my eyesight dead ahead on the frozen lake. My poor legs were carrying me as fast as they could, and it made me wish I had stayed in real school and took gym classes.

My thoughts scrambled as I ran, distracting myself from reality. Then Harriet stepped into my view. I got past all the cabins, but I couldn't slow down fast enough not to run into her.

"Oof!" We both fell down, but I rolled over and immediately got up to start running again. Harriet, fast as she was, caught up to me.

"K! What happened?! I heard a gunshot! You said he wouldn't shoot!"

"It's fine, he missed!" I grabbed her hand and we sprinted onto the frozen lake. From behind us, we heard a loud bellow.

"YOU CAN'T KEEP RUNNING, LAKE!" Roman hollered, his voice echoing across the barren lake.

"MY LEGS STILL WORK, SO YES I CAN!"

Harriet hit my arm. "DON'T PROVOKE HIM, DUMBASS!"

I looked back as our feet continued to meet the ice at a rapid pace, trying my best not to slip. Abe was running right behind Roman, but he tripped and fell. He called out in pain for his boyfriend, prompting both our chaser and Harriet to stop dead in their tracks. As Roman raced back to Abe, I skidded to a halt once I realized Harriet stopped, my boots scratching on the ice.

"Harriet, we have to—"

"Just wait, please." She begged, her eyebrows twisting in concern.

When Roman reached his arm out, instead of getting up, Abe forcefully pulled him down and took his gun. He aimed it at a pile of snow near the end of the ice and shot it three times, the sound of the shots booming. Before he could shoot the last bullet, Roman snatched it back.

"Abe! What the hell?!"

"You said we weren't going to hurt anyone! Especially not Harriet!" Abe screamed back at him, trying to grab the gun again. Roman kept it out of his reach and ran away, storming towards us. Harriet and I stopped to make sure Abe was okay, wondering what would happen next. We didn't start running again. I couldn't keep running.

I squeezed Harriet's hand, then opened it and placed my car keys onto her palm. "Harriet. Go help your brother and get out of here."

"No. I'm not leaving you alone like this."

"I'm not alone. Go."

Roman drew closer and closer. Harriet stepped in front of me when he pointed his gun, one bullet remaining.

"No." She shook her head. She wasn't even slightly scared by the gun, which was both the bravest and dumbest thing I had ever seen.

"Harriet, get out of the way," Roman commanded.

"An eye for an eye and the world goes blind, Roman. I'm not letting you hurt K."

"This doesn't involve you! GET OUT OF THE WAY!" His eyes were deranged and manic, but mostly scared.

I recognized those eyes. Seeing them… calmed me. My shoulders relaxed, and I found myself gazing into his green orbs as if they would give me all the answers.

"You involved me when you TOOK MY BROTHER AWAY! K did some horrible shit, no one's denying that! But your revenge is so fucking stupid! You two are GODS and you're acting like CHILDREN!"

"Um… Guys?" Abe called from behind but was ignored.

"This all started with Lake! She's the one who—"

I snapped back into reality, glaring at him. "I'm the one trying to put an end to all this!"

"YOU DON'T GET TO DECIDE WHEN IT ENDS!" He yelled and yelled, all the anger he had boiling up becoming seemingly uncontrollable. I was bored of it, so I rolled my eyes and looked away. My eyes drifted all over, anywhere but at him. The screaming Roman directed specifically at me becoming nothing more than white noise. Eventually, my eyes landed on Abe.

We stood quite a few feet away from him. He stared down at the ice, his stance wide. Looking up at us, he eyed Roman desperately. But Roman was far too focused on yelling at me to notice his struggling boyfriend.

I was surprised how long it took me to figure out why Abe looked so panicked, but when he took a small step forward and a long, loud, snapping elastic sound echoed around the lake, I didn't even need to look down at the crack beneath my feet to understand.

My eyes widened, and I reached my hand out to him. "STOP!" I yelped.

Roman, who had now gone to bickering with Harriet, jerked his head towards me. "Shut up! I'll deal with you—"

"Don't take another step!" I moved out from behind Harriet and watched Abe. He looked up at me, then back at the ice. The white lines in the ice were spreading, the same elastic-snapping, cracking sound echoing across the lake and through everyone's ears.

Roman finally took his head out of his ass and looked over at Abe, who gave him a pleading look.

"Abe..." He took a few steps toward his love, stepping on a crack and making it expand like an ever-growing tree branch.

"Stop!" I commanded.

He looked at me and glared, daggers in his stare. "You didn't stop when I begged you to stop slitting my wrists, why should I?"

"Roman, please."

He decided to ignore me and walked towards Abe anyway, ice cracking with each step he took. I swiftly ran up to him, grabbing his arm and pulling him back. "You need to listen to me, and I'll tell you exactly why."

He violently lashed his arm out of my grip, his dark eyes narrowing. "Oh, yeah?"

"You should listen to me because I'm right."

He rolled his eyes, "You're insufferable—"

"But I wasn't right." I interrupted. "I wasn't. I wasn't right when I tried to leave you, and I wasn't right when I killed you. I was an idiot, I was wrong, and I was selfish. I can't understand your pain, and I'm so, so sorry I put you through all that. I used to think I had excuses for what I did, but I don't. I was selfish like you said. You were right, Roman. And, Harriet was right too. I'm done being defensive about my mistakes. We betrayed Her and it got us turned into humans, and even though you were the only one who stayed by my side, I acted like immature and took my anger and fear out on you." I glanced at Abe, who was barely being held up by the ice. "You don't have to forgive me, but at least listen to me so I can help Abe."

He didn't respond. He said nothing. His eyes were lost in confusion and his mouth was slightly ajar as if he wasn't sure if what he just heard was real.

I turned to Abe. "Slowly sit down on the ice."

He hesitantly stared at us, then the ice.

"Do what she says, Abe," Roman assured him and took centimeter long steps towards him, barely crawling along to get closer.

He gently nodded. He looked from Roman to the ice and started slowly lowering his stance. When he got one knee onto the ice, it cracked more.

"Abe, be careful!" Harriet warned from behind us. I went to grab her hand and comfort her, but the ice under Abe started to make a horrible, twisted, snapping noise. I watched as the crystal underneath him caved in, and he fell into the black water under the glassy ice.

Thinking back to it, the scene reminded me of all those times I'd watched a planet be decimated by a black hole. Whenever we were bored of a planet we'd created, we would just destroy it, all the inhabitants going down with it. I never cared about them, though. They didn't matter. Why would they? Eventually, they would die whether it was by our hands or not.

I only realized that they mattered when I found out I could die too, furthering my selfishness. Soon, the weight of all the lives I had given and taken away finally settled in my cognition.

But at that moment, I wasn't thinking about my mortality, the planets I'd made, or even the ones I'd destroyed. I wasn't thinking at all. I didn't have time to, because as soon as Abe fell through the ice, I jumped in after him.

Chapter 10

My insides felt colder than the icy parts of the underworld, yet my skin was warm to the touch. My arms shivered down to my fingertips, and I felt waves of numbness followed by needles all over my body. My eyelids slowly drifted open, but all I saw was a bright, blinding light. I recoiled because of it, moving my hand to shade my eyes, but something pink came into my blurry view.

"K! K, can you hear me? You didn't lose your hearing, did you?" The blob of pale pink and peach looked off to the side. "That can happen, right?"

I stretched my arms out and latched onto the side of the couch I was resting on, weakly pulling myself up. "Harriet…?" I questioned, my voice cracking like glass. There was a dip in the couch next to me and a sudden hand on my shoulder.

"How are you feeling, K?"

"… Cold."

"Yeah, I kind of expected that…"

My vision faded back in bit by bit, and I took in my surroundings to help compose myself. I

stared out a dark window, noticing the juxtaposition of the warm interior next to the cold and harsh outside. Sharp wind whistled past the familiar oak walls of the cabin as it shielded us from a vicious snow storm.

The pink blob from before, that I could now identify as Harriet, scooted closer to me and put her head on my shoulder.

I glanced at her as she leaned back against the couch and held onto my arm, keeping her head comfortingly on my shoulder. "What happened…? I don't remember much…"

"You jumped into a frozen lake."

"… Sounds uncharacteristic."

"It was to save my brother."

"… Still sounds uncharacteristic."

"I fell in, so you jumped in after me," a short figure with purple hair said as he sat down on the coffee table in front of us, "So, thank you."

I glanced up at the freckled boy and nodded. "It's all part of the job, I suppose." My bones ached because of how hard I shivered, and I let a whimper escape.

"Oh no… Hold on, I'll get you more blankets and make some tea." Harriet's gentle grip on my arm left as she got up and left, leaving me and Abe alone.

I ran a hand through my hair and straightened my back, cracking my back as I stretched. "Where's Roman?" I inquired mid-stretch.

"He has a habit of not sleeping for days, and he didn't at all this week, so I made him take a nap. I'm hoping it'll last until morning…"

"Mmm… Old habits die hard."

"He did that in other lives too?"

A small smile curved its way into my lips. "All the time. I would wake up and find him staring at the stars, completely lost in thought."

"… I think he misses home…"

"We all do. Or, we did. Who's to say how many of us there are left."

"Lake… Did you ever really love Roman?"

My eyebrow raised at the intent of his query. "Excuse me?"

"Oh, I'm sorry. I didn't mean for it to sound that accusatory… He has this… this weird complex as if I'm going to betray him or leave him or something. And sometimes he acts like I don't actually love him. I just wanted to know… If you… You know. I know the whole story between you two, but only his side. So… I was just wondering."

"I was in love with him far before we were turned into humans," I answered factually. "It was a love that lasted centuries, lifetimes, and eternities. And I never thought love like that could fade. But it did."

His fingers glided up and down his arm as his stare awkwardly drifted towards the floor, feeling the tension in the room not drift away as we both so hoped that it would.

"But," I turned to face him fully, "I'm glad he found someone else he loves."

Turned to me as well as his smile matched mine.

"So, how did you react to the immortal god thing?" I asked with a chuckle, hoping to lighten the mood further.

His head tilted back to let out a laugh. "I actually took it rather well. I was barely even surprised when he told me."

"Really? Your sister freaked out."

His hand slipped through his hair. "Yeaaah… Well, I know Roman much better than she does, and this generation has basically grown up on the idea of immortals. There're songs, movies, books, even video games based on immortal people. I figured they'd be a part of my life eventually."

"Your generation is extremely strange."

He grinned cheekily. "I can't wait to see what the next generation is like."

The rest of the night was filled with low laughter and slowly emptying teacups. Our laughter died eventually, as did our energy. Abe stayed in the bedroom with Roman, and Harriet gladly rested next to me on the large, creaky couch. Her arm flopped over my stomach as she sweetly cuddled up to my side.

"K…?"

"Yes?"

"Thanks for helping me find my brother."

I tucked a small strand of hair behind her ear. "He wasn't lost."

"… I'm sorry for betraying you."

My eyes closed, and I released a brief sound of annoyance. "No. Stop that. I hate apologies."

"No, you don't. You hate the concept of apologies."

"Exactly. They're the proof of human imperfections. They're proof that humans can damage one another easily, but a lack of apologies is almost worse. I despise thinking about all the things in the world that need to be apologized for, too. Humans… And I mean this with absolutely no offense, suck.

She snickered. "No, you're right. Humans are the worst. But not always. Sometimes they're really nice."

"The nice ones never feel human, though."

"That's true. Maybe no one's a human. Maybe that's what 'She' was trying to create when She made us."

My lips curved, grinning like a fool. "Maybe."

I let my mind succumb to unconsciousness.

My darkness was interrupted by cold wind tickling the back of my neck. My hips slipped under the covers slowly as I replaced my body with pillows for Harriet to cuddle up to. I limped closer to the window, my eyes immediately focusing on the dark-haired boy standing on the porch in the cold.

"Dumbass…" I huffed quietly, searching around the room. When I opened the door to join him outside, my arms were full of blankets.

"Hey, stranger." The sound of the door opening startled him, and his foot almost slipped on some ice as he took a defensive stance. I chuckled. "You can relax, it's me."

"That's what I was afraid of."

I draped a few blankets over his shoulders and took a spot next to him, leaning against the porch banister.

"Have you spoken to Abe…? How is he feeling?" He inquired, adjusting the blankets over his shoulders.

"He seemed fine. He'll most likely catch a cold or flu, as will I, but he's fine."

"Thank God…"

I chuckled. "I don't think She had anything to do with this."

"It's just an expression…"

"Right."

The cumbersome tension made itself annoyingly known, taking over the conversation and my thoughts. My mind was far too filled with comments about awkwardness and discomfort that I didn't notice Roman staring at me.

"What?"

"Why did you save Abe?" His face tensed with this sad, lost expression.

"Excuse me?"

"Why did you jump in and save him? You could have just told me he was about to fall, and I would have done it."

"… Wait, are you jealous that I saved your boyfriend before you could, or are you genuinely curious why I would try and save a person?"

He groaned, "No, I didn't mean it like… You've always been selfish. I think today was the very first time I ever heard you apologize genuinely to someone. So why would you jump in after him and put yourself at risk? You could have easily told me, and I would have done it."

"Well, you had a gun and were in a slight rampage - no offense. I doubt you would have believed me. You would have thought it was just me trying to distract you. Besides, I wasn't thinking. I saw he was in trouble and jumped in… That pun wasn't intended but now that I hear it, I'm embracing it."

He laughed and slowed it to a chuckle. He kept on chuckling, and chuckling, and chuckling.

"Come on, it wasn't that funny—" I turned to Roman and saw his shoulders shaking as tears dropped from his eyes. The remnants of his chuckle turned slowly into sobs. "Oh, Roman… I'm sorry, I didn't think that would offend you. I didn't me—"

"I'm so sorry, Lake." He sobbed louder. "I was so in love with you... I already felt so alone. I didn't want to lose you, and I ended up driving you away. You were everything to me for so long." His head fell into his hands as his shoulders shook violently.

"You don't have to apologize…" I looked at him, knowing we were in the same boat. But we couldn't agree who was captain. We couldn't agree who got us into this storm in the first place.

I glanced towards the snow in the air, watching the clumps of frost disappear into piles of its kind. "I know it's immature, but I wish I could just forget all of it happened."

He nodded meekly.

"Well… I wish I could forget the bad parts, like hurting you and hiding. I don't want to forget anything else."

My throat seized at the uncomfortable thought of saying anything more. There had been too many emotional talks today and I couldn't handle another. My mind and eyes wandered above me, towards the stars. The small specs of light in the sky that shined through gaps in clouds caught my attention. How could they not?

"We really did a good job when we made those, didn't we? They're beautiful from Earth."

He looked to me, then up. "The stars…? Yeah… We did do a good job…" He sniffled, wiping away the last of his tears. "But you did a much better job with the moon."

I chuckled under my breath. "Remember when Ora made the sun? He was so proud of himself. He kept bragging about it, and when we told him he just stole our idea for the stars and made an orange version, he got all mad and told us we stole the idea from his mind."

"And then eeeeveryone wanted to make a different type of star." He snickered.

"Remember how Scorpius wanted all the zodiacs to be named after her?"

"Yes! She didn't even understand that it would get confusing if they were all the same name!"

"It's like naming everything Earth! "Hi, Earth, how is Earth? Great! How is Earth going? That's Earthy!"

I laughed loudly, gently bending over the rail and clutching my stomach. Roman chuckled along with me and kept a happy smile on his face.

He took a deep breath, lips stilled curved. "All of our friends are dead."

I turned around, directly in view of the window. I gazed at Harriet calmly sleeping, not a care, undisturbed by the world's issues. "Not all of them."

I smiled at him sweetly. "Now, come on, it's very late. We should be asleep."

His hair bounced as he nodded his head, then lifted it up to the stars. Nostalgia washed over me, watching the way the sky reflected in his eyes like another universe. I had seen this exact image a thousand different times, in a thousand different lifetimes, and I didn't realize I missed it until I felt a hole in my soul be filled.

"Yeah, Lake… You're right."

Chapter 11

I removed the nozzle from my car's tank, hanging it back by its handle. My eyes shifted towards the busy road, only to watch someone saunter up to me.

"Hey." A friendly, familiar voice greeted. I gazed at the source of the voice. I was surprised but cheery.

"Harriet!" A smile tugged on my lips, stepping closer to her. "How are you? What are you doing here?"

"One of my parents' skating rinks is right there," she pointed behind her at a brightly lit outdoor skating rink just across the street. "And since they own the place, we get in for free."

On the mostly barren ice, two just as familiar boys skated around. One slipped, and the other simply laughed instead of helping him up.

I sniggered at them before focusing back on Harriet. "I was sure you three would have enough of ice."

"No," a grin formed on her lips, "we love skating too much. Anyway, your apartment is

nowhere near here. Are you leaving town or something?"

"Now look who's the detective. Giving me a run for my money, huh?"

She rolled her eyes, her grin static.

"Yeah, I'm, uh, I'm going to visit my dad for his birthday. I owe him at least that."

Her grin visibly softened, turning into a calm, gentle, and amused look. "That's good. I'm glad. I hope it goes well."

"Thank you. How are they doing…? Roman and Abe? It was a few weeks ago, so I assume fine?"

"Pretty much. Roman has been over at our house every day since he "missed Abe so much while he was on his trip"."

"Ah, so your parents still aren't aware of what really happened."

"Nope. Don't think they ever will be. It's not something you can just… explain casually and, move on like everything's fine. Anyway, Abe and Roman have been acting as in love as ever." She chuckled. "And… Abe and I came out to our parents."

"Oh." My eyes widened, and my eyebrows curved, almost concerned. It seemed like a secret she was determined to keep forever. "How did it go?"

"A lot better than we thought. They were confused, but we explained all of it as best as we could and told them about Roman. Surprisingly, they were super relieved Abe was going out with Roman and not 'some creep'."

I attempted my best not to laugh, I really did, but I ended up letting out a choked snicker. "A tad ironic."

"A tad."

I finished the exchange of gas for money and bought two hot chocolates. Handing one to Harriet, she suggested I come hang out with her and the lovebirds for a while. I agreed, and I drove us both over to the skating rink.

Harriet put her skates back on and headed onto the ice again. Her hair whipped over her shoulders as she twirled in front of me on her skates, then promptly slipped and fell on her ass. I giggled teasingly, watching her get up.

She gave me nothing but a dirty look. "I'd love to see you try." She extended her arms to

balance herself, then skated closer and took her hot chocolate from next to me on the edge of the rink.

"So…" She slowly sipped it, "What are you going to do from now on?"

"Occupation wise? Stay on my current path. At least for now. Maybe I'll go back to university, try something else. I'm not sure what I want to do in my next life, so maybe I can try and figure it out now."

"Hm. Sounds like a good plan."

Harriet abruptly began avoiding my gaze. Her expression was not at all guilty, or even sad. It was indecisive, as though she had something to say but the words were scrambled, and she couldn't quite put them back together. Once she found her words, she retained eye contact.

"So... Like... Weird question, but... what was your first memory? Like, from the very beginning of your existence. Or birth. Or however gods work."

"That's an interesting question... I don't think I know my real first memory, but I can recall my oldest memory; my name. Gods aren't born the same way humans are since they tend to just... pop into existence, so, Her giving me my name is, technically speaking, my first memory."

"What was your first memory as a human?"

"Well... Human memories are much hazier than god memories, mostly because most of my lives were countless repetitions. Life after life, Roman and I did almost the same thing, over and over. In turn, my memories all collided and turned into... somewhat of an amalgamation."

"I'm just going to pretend I know what that means."

"It's a strange way of saying a fusion."

"Oh. Cool… Do you like being a human…?"

"I don't hate it, but I'd be lying if I said I didn't miss being a god. At least I have a little more power than a regular human, with the whole reincarnation ability."

"So, you don't think humans are reincarnated?"

My shoulders lifted, and I gave her an unsure look. "Not in the same way Roman and I are. I think something about every human lives on, whether it's in their children, other loved ones, or what they created. Every human

leaves something of importance behind, and because of that, I think that whenever that thing is re-used, or when that loved one exhibits traits of the past human, something about them is reborn. Maybe not physically, but in memory, and in spirit."

Harriet was silent for a moment, almost surprised by my response, but then she just laughed and punched my arm. "You're such a nerd."

I stuck my tongue out at her but didn't break my ear-to-ear smile. "Whatever, weirdo."

Harriet glanced behind her, watching Abe and Roman, who glided around the ice together, hand in hand. "Are you and Roman good now…? I know that kind of thing isn't really forgiven easily, but…"

"Yeah, I'm... I'm pretty sure we're good now. At least I hope we are."

"Well, he hasn't been scheming to destroy you and torture you forever recently, so that's a start."

I almost fell off the edge of the rink in laughter. "Yeah, that's definitely a start!" Happily glancing down, I noticed my watch and quickly checked the time. "Whoa, I really need to get going..."

She frowned, skating closer to me. "Aw... Really?"

"Yeah... It's getting late. I'd prefer not to fall asleep at the wheel."

"It's only, like, 9 o'clock." She giggled.

I stuck my tongue out at her. "Some people like not being sleep deprived, you know."

She laughed, "Okay, okay, let me get my boots and I'll walk you back to your car."

After retrieving her boots and slipping them on again, Harriet clasped her hand around mine and we wandered back to my car.

"So, promise you'll actually answer my texts next time?" She crossed her arms sassily, clearly annoyed by our lack of communication.

I bit the inside of my cheek and smiled. "Yeah, I'm sorry about that… I was dealing with another few cases. They've been piling up rather quickly lately."

"Well, you've been solving mysteries since before the dawn of time… You've got this."

She pulled a small piece of hair out of my face, tucking it behind my ear sweetly. Her hand glided down my face and onto my cheek.

My cold cheek rushed with blood and heated up rapidly. "Thank, you Harriet…"

Her foot stepped forward, moving closer to me. "Just promise you won't be so busy you won't have time to come skating with me."

I put my finger under her chin and nodded gently. "I promise." My eyes fluttered close as I leaned closer and pressed my lips sweetly against her own. I felt her lips curve happily as she kissed back.

I pulled back after a moment, watching Harriet eyes flip open and light up brightly. She giggled and gently bit her lip. "I'll see you around, K- or, Lake, or..."

"Kira."

"Kira?"

"It's my birth name," I said, gazing at her lovingly.

A smile tugged further at her lips. "Oh. Okay. Well, then, I'll see you around, Kira."

My lungs filled, making me feel the butterflies that had formed. I kissed her forehead. "I hope so."

Harriet headed back to rejoin her brother and friend, and I drove out of the parking lot, rounding the corner and passing the ice rink again. Abe, Harriet, and Roman gathered around the end of the ice and were waving at me. My eyes met Roman's familiar ones, who after a moment, smiled benevolently at me. Smiling back, I felt everything let go. Every fear, every grudge, every bit of anger, sadness, or grief. And without all that negativity crowding my head and making me drown, I took a deep breath and simply did what I loved.

I drove.

South VC, 2019

Made in the USA
Las Vegas, NV
24 January 2021

16463653R00069